Usborne
10 Ten-Minute
Bedtime Stories

Usborne
10 Ten-Minute
Bedtime Stories

CONTENTS

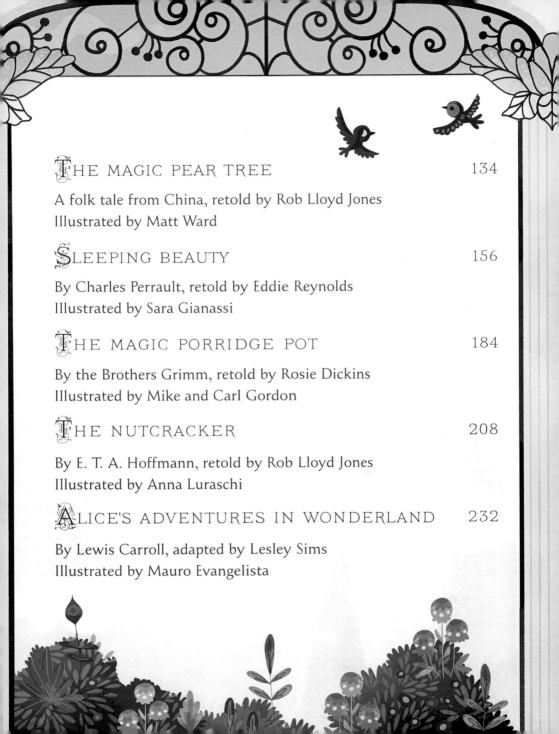

CINDERELLA

Along, long time ago, an unhappy girl named
Cinderella lived a miserable life. Every day,
she scrubbed and scoured, fixed and fetched from
dawn until dusk. She had no friends, and no one
ever had a kind word to say to her.

Although Cinderella slaved all day, her sour-faced stepmother and spoiled step-sisters complained about everything she did. Cinderella never complained and she never got cross.

Every night, exhausted, she went to sleep by the fire. In her dreams she remembered the happy days when her father and mother were still alive.

Every morning, she woke up in the same sooty kitchen, with the same sore back and the same never-ending list of chores. Nothing ever changed.

Until one morning, when a letter arrived...

"Saints alive!" gasped her stepmother as she read the letter. "It's from the king, girls! Every eligible woman in the kingdom is invited to a ball...and... Oh my goodness! "

"What-what-what?" screeched the step-sisters.

"At the ball, the prince will choose...his bride!"

"The prince!" For the next two months, as
Cinderella sewed their dresses for the ball, all the
step-sisters could do was squabble about which of
them the prince was going to marry.

At last, the big day arrived. Of course, no one imagined that Cinderella was going to the party.

"Don't forget to scrub the toilets!" cried her step-sisters as their carriage rolled away.

Cinderella went back to the kitchen and sobbed. Life was so unfair.

Suddenly, with a noise like a bubble popping backwards, a strange lady appeared in the kitchen.

"Dry your tears! I am your fairy godmother," she explained in a silvery voice. "You are a kind girl and I want to make you very happy."

Cinderella was startled, but she knew at once what she wanted.

"Please may I go to the ball?" she asked.

"A fine idea!" grinned the fairy. "First, please find me your biggest pumpkin. I'll also need... yes, those mice and that rat in the trap..."

Cinderella was worried that the woman was crazy, but she did exactly as she was told.

The fairy godmother skipped into the garden.

"Pumpkin-bumpkin! Sprout a new skin!" she sang and waved her wand.

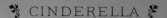

With a groaning noise the pumpkin began to swell and bulge. To Cinderella's astonishment, it grew into an elegant carriage.

"Mice! Thrice! Hoofitty splice!"

With a swish of the fairy's wand, the mice became six dancing, prancing horses.

"Hmm, you'll need some footmen." The fairy glanced around the garden. "Aha! Those lizards will do!" She waved her wand again and... PING!

Next, **POW**! The rat became a coachman. "This is the best part," giggled the fairy. "My dear, we're going to make you fabulous!"

She wrapped Cinderella in soft shivers of golden silk and put dainty glass slippers on her feet.

"You look wonderful, Cinderella," said the fairy. "But you must be back by midnight or all my charms will fade away. Please don't forget!"

"How can I ever repay you?" asked Cinderella.

"By having fun! Dance well, my dear!"

Cinderella sped to the castle. Swirling music,
sparkling lights and rich scents filled the air with
magic. She took a deep breath on the stairs. She
couldn't quite believe this was happening.

When Cinderella entered the ballroom, everything stopped. No one could take their eyes off the mysterious stranger. Then the whispers started. "Who is she?" "Such grace!" "What style!"

The prince quickly rushed to greet her. "Might I have the next dance?" he asked. "Of course, your highness," replied Cinderella.

The golden pair glided across the ballroom. They were so happy together and danced so well, it looked as if they'd known each other forever.

The prince refused to dance with anyone else.

"It's not fair!" sneered one of the step-sisters. "This clumsy upstart is hogging the prince!"

"The prince is a mutton-head!" complained the other. "We're the most beautiful ladies at this ball!"

Neither the prince nor Cinderella
wanted the night to end. They
laughed and chatted and danced
and lost all track of time.
Suddenly, Cinderella heard
a clock strike midnight.
"Oh no!" she cried.
"I have to go!"

"Wait!" shouted the prince.

Cinderella didn't stop. She was terrified that her secret would be discovered.

Her clothes were already changing back to rags. She stumbled and lost a glass slipper on the stairs.

Limping, she took off the other slipper. But time had run out for her coach and horses.

"Come back!" called the prince, "Please! I don't even know your name."

Hiding in a bush, Cinderella dared not reply. The prince returned to his ball, broken-hearted.

"Did you have fun?" asked Cinderella, when her step-sisters arrived home.

"It was SO boring," said one step-sister.

"And the prince is ugly and rude," said the other.

"Run us a bath at once!" they shouted.

The next morning, trumpets sounded from the castle and the prince began a tour of every house in the kingdom.

"I want to find the woman who fits this shoe," he explained. "So I can marry her."

They visited house after house, with no luck. At last, they arrived at Cinderella's front door. When the prince knocked, Cinderella's stepmother sent her from the room.

Both the sisters swore that the shoe was theirs, but no matter how much they pushed and strained, it simply wouldn't fit.

The prince spotted Cinderella hiding in the next room. "Would you like to try?" he asked.

"Of course she can't!" snapped her step-mother. "Ignore her. She's useless."

But the prince insisted. "Everyone must try," he said.

Naturally, the slipper was a perfect fit. Even better, Cinderella still had the other slipper in her pocket. She pulled it out and everyone gasped.

"I am so happy that I found you," said the prince.

There was a tinkle of laughter and the sound of a bubble popping backwards.

Suddenly, Cinderella was wrapped in starlight and moonbeams. She looked magnificent.

"This is the best day of my life," said the prince. "Will you marry me?"

"Yes!" Cinderella smiled, as her sisters scowled.

Cinderella and the prince were married the next day. Cinderella was so kind that she forgave her awful family, and she and the prince lived and loved happily ever after.

THE GOLDEN GOOSE

nce there was a woodcutter, who had three sons, Andy, Dandy and Sandy. The oldest, Andy, was the biggest and the strongest, just as strong as his father – or maybe even stronger.

Andy could already chop up a gigantic tree and carry the logs home in ten minutes.

Dandy didn't care about being strong. He was extremely handsome. So he simply admired himself...a lot.

Sandy wasn't strong or handsome, but he was kind and always remembered to feed the family pets.

One morning, the woodcutter couldn't get out
of bed. His face was a revolting shade of mustard
yellow and his body was shivery.

"Andy, you'll have to cut down all the trees on
your own today," he croaked.

"Of course, Father!" Andy replied. Secretly, he
thought he was a much better woodcutter anyway.

That day, Andy chopped
the wood in double-quick
time, so he could get on
with his lunch.

Just as he was
unwrapping his
delicious pie, a
funny little man
appeared. "May
I have some?"

"No!" snapped Andy, "I'm
very hungry. I need it all!"
   "Is that so?" said the
funny little man, and
vanished...

When he got home, Andy started his exercise routine. He liked to do a few thousand press-ups every night. And one, two, three...but ARGH! Red spots burst out all over his body.

"Oh, I do hope that isn't catching," said Dandy.

To Dandy's horror, the next day he had to go in his father's place. Andy's spots were very itchy and he was too busy scratching them to chop wood.

Dandy started to chop down a tree, but it made him hot and sweaty. Oh no! Sweat would make his lovely curls frizzy! Dandy pulled out his hand mirror to check.

"I should sit down, rest and recuperate," thought Dandy. "It's probably lunch time." He was putting on his napkin when a funny little man interrupted him.

"Oo, could I share your lunch?"

"I made this especially for my delicate digestion," said Dandy. "It's not meant for ordinary, unattractive people, I'm afraid."

But before he'd finished speaking, the man had mysteriously disappeared.

That night, Dandy was brushing his hair one hundred times and putting in his curlers, when... ARGH! His skin was purple!

"What's happened to my flawless skin?"

Andy and Sandy came running to see what was happening. Andy started laughing.

"Do you need anything, Dandy?" asked Sandy.

"DON'T TOUCH ME!"
Dandy screamed. "I'll try
one of my special ointments.
But you're going to have to
work tomorrow, Sandy!"

"All right," said Sandy. He didn't know how to be a woodcutter, but he was going to try his best.

After a slow morning's work, Sandy had taken one bite out of his sandwich, when...

"Oooo, may I have a nibble?"

It was the funny little man.

"Of course," Sandy said, passing him the sandwich.

"Thank you very much," said the
funny little man. "Now, see this tree?
Why don't you chop it down next?"

Sandy glanced up at the tree.
It looked just like the others.

"Okay then," he said, looking back
to the man...but he was gone.

Sandy started sawing.
He sawed and sawed
until... CRASH!

The tree was not at all like
the others. Inside, Sandy found
a golden goose.

"That's odd," said Sandy, "I
suppose I should take you home."

But soon it was dark, and the goose was heavy. Sandy wandered around, getting more and more lost. In the distance, he saw an inn with glowing windows.

"Hello, sir," Sandy said to the innkeeper. "May my goose and I have a bed for the night?"

The innkeeper's daughters stared, hypnotized by the gleaming feathers of the golden goose.

After his long and
strange day, Sandy was
soon snoring in bed,
still clutching the goose.
Silently, the oldest daughter crept in.

She plucked at one of the goose's beautiful
golden feathers, but her fingers stuck fast! Her
sisters stared at her, horrified, as she tugged and
tugged to free herself.

"Help me, oh,
one of you help
meeeeee!" she screeched.

The middle sister grabbed hold of her skirt
and the youngest sister pulled the middle
sister's dress.

"What's happening?" yawned Sandy, woken by
the kerfuffle.

"We're stuck,"
said the youngest
sister. "We're all
stuck to your
golden goose."

"Oh dear," said Sandy. "Well, if I move over I think we can all fit in my bed and sort it out in the morning." They did all fit, but no one slept very well, not even the goose. In fact, especially not the poor goose who was the smallest and so the most easily squashed.

"Maybe I can find that funny little man and he can sort this," thought Sandy. He set off, with the goose tucked under his arm and the innkeeper's three daughters trailing behind him.

"Wait, where do you think you're going?" shouted the girls' mother. She caught hold of her youngest daughter's skirt and immediately became stuck too.

"What's going on out here? What's all this rumpus?" shouted the innkeeper as he raced outside.

"We're stuck!" everyone yelled back.

"How can you be stuck? How silly," huffed the innkeeper.

He marched up to his wife and tugged hard on her apron...and he was stuck as well. "Oh," he said, sheepishly.

"Wuff," said his dog.

And so the three daughters, their mother and their father followed Sandy and his goose. Wherever he went, they went too, just like a train made of people. The train chugged all the way to a castle.

The king lived there with his daughter, the sad Princess Fleur. She was famous throughout the kingdom, because she had never, ever laughed. It wasn't Fleur's fault. Her life just wasn't very funny.

She went to lots of dull royal
engagements with lots and lots
of boring princes who only talked
about themselves.

So when Princess Fleur looked
out of her window and saw
Sandy, she felt something odd.
It bubbled up inside her throat.
It bubbled and bubbled. Fleur
tried to cover her mouth, but
the laughter exploded out.

"Fleur, are you unwell?" the king asked. Fleur couldn't reply. She laughed for so long, she could barely stand up.

"Father, that boy and the goose...and the people... I've never seen anything so funny in my entire life," Fleur gasped, when she had finally recovered herself.

"You, the boy with the goose," boomed the king, "How can I thank you? I know – a party!"

The trouble was, they were all still stuck to Sandy's golden goose. But, just then, the funny little man appeared, holding a present.

"Hello, Sandy," he said, "I've brought you a gift for the party." He tapped the box with his stick. Magic shot out into the air, covering Sandy, the goose and the others, and then...at last...they came unstuck.

Not only did everyone come unstuck, but Andy, Dandy and their father appeared – all completely recovered. Now everyone could enjoy the party, especially the golden goose, who much preferred life without people hanging off its feathers.

THE WIZARD OF OZ

Out among the rolling plains and broad skies of Kansas, a girl named Dorothy lived on a lonely farm with her Aunt Em, her Uncle Henry and her little dog, Toto.

Sometimes, the wind howled over the farm with fearsome force, whirling around and around. One day, a storm came which whirled the farmhouse right up into the air – with Dorothy and Toto inside it.

The house sailed through the sky for hours...then landed with a tooth-jolting CRUNCH.

Dorothy peeked outside and saw some strange-looking people in pointy hats. "Welcome to the Land of Oz," they cried, bowing to her. "And thank you!"

"You have killed the Wicked Witch of the East and set us free."

"W-w-what?" stammered Dorothy, feeling confused. "I haven't killed anyone!"

"It was your house, dear," explained a kind-looking woman. "Look down there!"

The woman took the witch's silver shoes and handed them to Dorothy. "These are yours now," she said. "Now, to get back home, you must go to see the Great Wizard of Emerald City. Just follow the yellow brick road..."

Dorothy set off, her new silver shoes tinkling on the bricks.

As she passed a cornfield, a scarecrow called out: "Hi there! Where are you going?"

Hello!

"To see the Great Wizard," replied Dorothy.

"Can I come?" said the scarecrow. "I'd like to ask the wizard for brains."

Dorothy nodded.

After a little while, Dorothy and the scarecrow came to a shadowy forest. In the leafy gloom, they heard a groan. A man made all of tin stood frozen by a pile of logs.

"Help!" he grunted. "I've rusted up."

Dorothy found an oil can. "We're off to see the wizard," she said, as she oiled his joints.

"Can I come?" asked the tinman. "I'd like to ask the wizard for a heart."

Thank you!

They had only gone a few steps when
a lion leaped out of the trees with an
ear-splitting RRR-ROAR! Toto yelped.

Bravely, Dorothy smacked the lion on
the nose. "Don't be a bully," she said.

"Sorry," mumbled the lion. "I only
wanted to ask, can I come with you? I'd
like to ask the wizard for some courage."

So Dorothy was joined not only by a
scarecrow and a tinman, but a lion as well.
The yellow brick road wound on and on,
past fields and rivers, and vast beds of silky
scarlet poppies. The poppies' heady scent
made Dorothy, Toto and the lion fall into
a deep slumber. But the tinman and the
scarecrow carried them on, past the
poppies, until they woke up again.

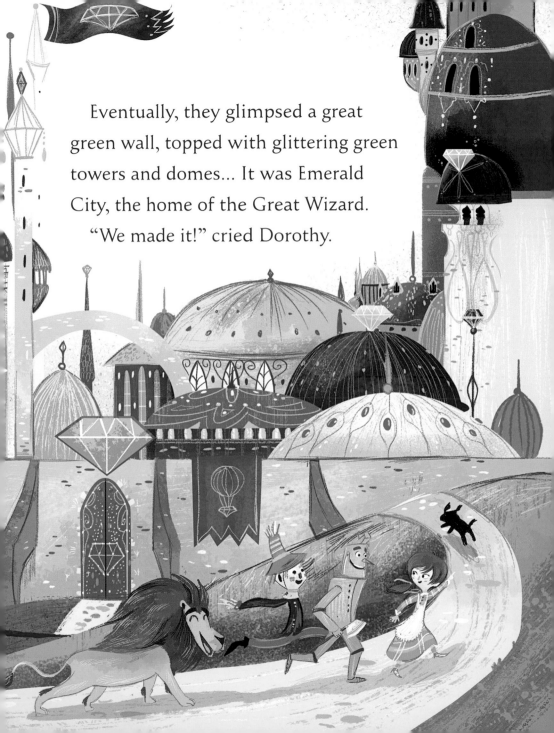

Eventually, they glimpsed a great
green wall, topped with glittering green
towers and domes... It was Emerald
City, the home of the Great Wizard.
"We made it!" cried Dorothy.

Before they were allowed through the city gates, they all had to put on green glasses, even Toto.

"It's for your eyes," explained the gatekeeper. "Our city is too dazzling without them!" Then he showed them inside – and they gasped.

There were green houses, and
green shops selling green candy.
EVERYTHING was green, even the sky.
The gatekeeper led them to the
Great Wizard's palace. "One at a time.
You first!" he told Dorothy.

Nervously, Dorothy creaked open a door and saw...a giant green head!

"I am the Great Wizard," it boomed. "What do you want?"

"Please, can you help me to go home to Kansas?" asked Dorothy.

"Only if you kill the Wicked Witch of the West!" boomed the reply.

Then the scarecrow stepped in...to be greeted by a winged lady. The tinman met a many-eyed monster, and the lion, a ball of fire. But whatever they saw, or asked for, each one received the same reply...

Kill the Wicked Witch!

There was nothing else to do but set off once more – this time for the witch's castle.

They walked by day and slept by night, journeying deeper into the west. But it is hard to catch a witch unawares, and the Wicked Witch of the West was no exception.

"So the wizard is sending you after me?" she hissed to herself. "We'll see about that..."

The witch summoned wild wolves and crows to attack the companions – but the scarecrow and tinman chased them away.

Then the witch put on a wishing cap and wished up a pack of flying monkeys. The monkeys flung the scarecrow and tinman into the wilds, and carried Dorothy, Toto and the lion to the witch.

"Ha! More slaves!" cackled the witch. She tied up the lion and set Dorothy to work scrubbing the floor.

The witch spotted Dorothy's beautiful shoes and tried to snatch them. Determined to stop her, Dorothy flung the pail of water she was carrying...

Take that!

At once, the witch began to shrink.

"I'm melting," she wailed. Soon, there was nothing left but some clothes lying in a puddle.

"She's gone," shouted Dorothy. "We're free!"

Now that the wishing cap was Dorothy's, it was easy to rescue her friends and return to the Great Wizard.

This time, they entered together – only to find an empty, echoing room. Then Toto barked at a screen, which fell over to reveal...a little old man!

"Who are you?" exclaimed the friends.

"I'm the wizard," he said. "You can call me Oz."

"What were those characters we saw before?"

"Um, they were tricks," admitted Oz. "Puppets. You see, I'm not a REAL wizard."

"But you promised to help us," insisted the friends. "We got rid of the witch."

Oz sighed. "I'll try. What do you seek?"

"Brains," said the scarecrow.

"A heart," added the tinman.

"Courage," whispered the lion.

"To go home," pleaded Dorothy.

Oz thought hard. "All right..."

First, Oz sewed a
handful of pins inside
the scarecrow's head.
"To make you
sharp!" he said.

For the tinman, there was a heart-shaped cushion,
and for the lion, a bottle marked 'Courage'.

Finally, Oz led Dorothy to a basket. "This is my balloon," he said. "Climb in. We'll fly you home!" He lit a fire and hot air began to swell the balloon.

Suddenly, Toto burst out barking and sprang from the basket. Dorothy dived after him.

Oh no!

Then a rope snapped and the balloon took off...

"Come back!" called Dorothy. But it was too late. The balloon was already too high.

"Now I'll NEVER get home," wept Dorothy. Her friends tried to comfort her.

"You still have the wishing cap," said the tinman gently.

So Dorothy picked it up and wished for the
flying monkeys. "Please," she begged, "can
you take me home to Kansas?"

"No," they replied. "Our magic
does not reach that far. But
we can take you to the
Good Witch Glinda.
Maybe she
can help."

Glinda lived in a glowing ruby castle. She welcomed the friends with a smile.

"How can I help you?" she asked.

Dorothy told her the whole story. "And now I just want to go home," she finished sadly. "Aunt Em will be so worried."

"May I have that cap?" asked Glinda.
"I will use it to send the scarecrow,
tinman and lion back to their homes.
As for you, Dorothy – your silver shoes
will take you home. Just knock the heels
together and wish."

Dorothy hugged her friends goodbye.
Then she held onto Toto tightly and
clicked her heels briskly together.

"Please take me home to Kansas!"
she cried. At once, she was whirling
through the air...

...and then running across a familiar field, towards her aunt – who gasped and caught her up in a warm, welcoming hug.

"Oh, Aunt Em," sighed Dorothy. "I've had such an adventure...but I'm SO glad to be home!"

THE WIND IN THE WILLOWS

Rat was taking his friend Mole for a trip in his boat, out on the river.

"There's nothing quite like it!" Rat beamed, as Mole clung to his paws and clambered aboard.

Rat wasn't wrong.

"My, oh my," said Mole, pointing in amazement, "to think I've spent my whole life underground... It's beautiful out here!"

Before Rat could respond, Otter's wet, brown head popped out of the water. "The river's busy this morning," he gasped. "Mr. Toad was out earlier, on his brand new barge."

This gave Rat an idea. "Let's pay Toad a visit!"

In no hurry at all, they drifted downstream until they reached Toad Hall.

"My, oh my..." said Mole, seeing Toad's grand mansion. It was at least fifty times bigger than the hole Mole called home.

They tied up the boat and strolled into the garden to find Toad outside, studying a map.

"Friends!" Toad cried. "Welcome! You're *just* in time for a trip in my new caravan."

"What about your new barge?" asked Rat, but Toad had already sped off to his stables.

Soon, Toad was driving his caravan, while Rat and Mole ambled happily alongside.

It felt good to be out on the open road.

Toad was boasting, as usual, this time about his magnificent horses, when **TOOT! TOOT!** a motor car swept past. The caravan crashed onto its side.

Rat was furious, but Toad was entranced.

"Oh Toad…" said Mole sadly, as he calmed down the horse. "Your caravan – it's ruined."

"What, that old cart?" Toad's reply surprised them both. "Who cares? I'm buying a motor car!"

And he talked of nothing else, all the way back to Toad Hall.

Rat was exhausted from their stressful day out. He took Mole home for tea, with a plan to relax, and do strictly nothing else, for at least two weeks.

But after only a few days, Mole grew bored. He wanted to carry on exploring the great outdoors. While Rat was snoozing, he set off alone...for the dark and mysterious Wild Woods.

Night fell so quickly that
Mole lost his way. Shadows
loomed over him. Strange moans and
rustles followed him from the trees above.
"Help! Somebody?" he cried, but no one heard.
Terrified and exhausted, he took shelter
inside the hollow of an old oak tree.

Back home, Rat had woken from a snooze and noticed that Mole's coat and boots were gone. Worried that his friend wouldn't find his way home, he set out to find him.

Mole was sobbing in his hollow, when he heard familiar cries. Relieved, he ran into Rat's arms. "Ratty, it's really you! What a scare I had."

On their way home, snow began to fall, covering the path. Mole feared they would have to spend an icy night outside...

...until he tripped on a door-scraper.

Ouch! What was that?

"Where there's a door-scraper, there's also a door," grinned Rat. "I think you've found Badger's house!" Badger had already heard them.

"Come in, you poor things," he chuckled. "You'll catch a cold out here!"

Inside, they basked by the crackling fire and ate a hearty supper of shortbread and cocoa.

"So Ratty, what's new?" Badger asked. "How's Toad these days?"

Rat sighed. "Dreadful! He's obsessed with his new car. He thinks he's the world's best driver, but I've heard he's crashed it three times already."

"Well," began Badger, "as all good friends should, we'll speak to him...but only once winter is over."

The next day, before waving goodbye, they agreed to meet in warmer weather.

True to his word, early the following spring, Badger arrived one morning while Mole and Rat were finishing their breakfast.

They marched to Toad Hall
to find Toad on his doorstep,
adjusting his driving goggles.

"Friends!" he guffawed. "You're
just in time for a drive..." He
paused as he noticed their frowns.

"Toad, we need to talk
about your driving," said
Badger, firmly.

Toad, insulted, refused to listen. The only way to stop him from driving was to lock him in his bedroom and take turns keeping watch.

Rat was on duty when Toad cried out. "Oh Ratty, please take pity. I feel ever so poorly. I need a doctor... Fast!"

Toad's voice was
certainly croakier
than usual, and
he could barely
keep his eyes
open. Worried, Rat
rushed into town
to find help.

"Ha, ha!" Toad
chuckled. Once Rat
was out of earshot,
he knotted his
bedsheets together,
then climbed down
from his window.
He'd escaped!

Giddy with excitement, Toad dashed into town. His eyes widened when he spotted a shiny, red car.

Oh, he knew that he shouldn't take it...

...but he knew that he could...

The next thing he knew, he had! The engine growled as he raced off at top speed.

The very next day, Toad was in court.

"Mr. Toad of Toad Hall," said the judge, sternly, "you are a thief. You stole a car and drove it dangerously. What's more, I am told you were rude to a policeman. I hereby sentence you to twenty years in prison!" The judge banged his gavel. His decision was final.

Please, have mercy!

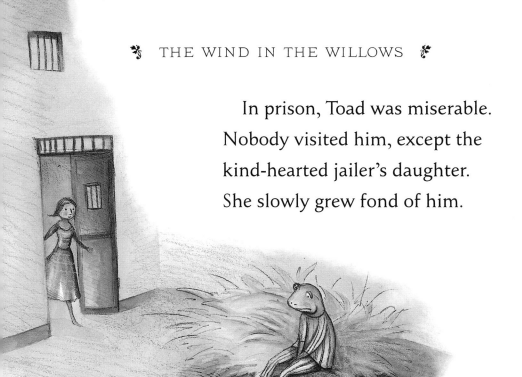

In prison, Toad was miserable. Nobody visited him, except the kind-hearted jailer's daughter. She slowly grew fond of him.

After weeks of trying to cheer him up, she knew there was only one way to make the lonely Toad happy.

So, one day, she handed him a pile of
unwashed clothes and a pink dress.
"I've had an idea," she said. "Try this
on." Puzzled, Toad scrambled into the
dress. "A perfect fit!" she giggled,
then whispered something in his ear.
Toad's eyes lit up.

That night, a short,
plump figure, almost
hidden behind a pile
of washing, crept from
the prison grounds.

Once again, he'd escaped!

"Toad, you're a genius." he
thought. "Brilliant plan and brilliant
washerwoman disguise. The guards
stood no chance."

The sun set, and the moon rose.
Toad rested against a tree and
dreamed sweet dreams of home.
Tomorrow, he'd be back in Toad Hall.

Toad was up with the sun. After four hours
of walking, he arrived at Toad Hall to find Rat
hiding behind a bush.

"Ratty?" he called. "What are you doing?"

Rat turned to him, alarmed.

"Toad! Ssshhh! The Weasels and
the Stoats have taken over Toad
Hall, and I'm spying on them!"

"But don't worry," Rat went on, "Badger's discovered a secret tunnel that will get us in to surprise them."

He led Toad to their den, where Badger explained his plan.

Late that night, they crept along the tunnel, weapons in hand, until Badger came to a halt. "We're here...here...here..." his voice echoed.

Above them was a trap door, leading into the kitchen. They scrambled up. The coast was clear. A rumpus of a racket was coming from the Dining Hall. Now was their chance to strike.

"CHARGE!" bellowed Badger, and they ran into the hall. Swords clanged. Plates shattered. Badger, Mole and Rat ran circles around the invaders. Toad made straight for the Chief Weasel and flung him from the table.

In less than five minutes, the battle was won.

"Dear, dear friends," Toad beamed. "We did it... And you're *just* in time for a party to celebrate!"

From that night on, Toad was no longer quite so brash and reckless, but happy simply to spend the time with his three best friends.

THE SNOW QUEEN

Once upon a time, Gerda and Kay were the best of friends. Every night, Gerda's grandma told them stories. Often, she warned of the wicked Snow Queen, who flew about the world in winter storms.

One evening, Kay thought he saw a beautiful woman staring at him through his window. When he peered closer, he felt a sharp scratch in his eye and a stab in his heart. Kay cried out in pain.

"What's wrong Kay," asked Gerda kindly.

"It's nothing," Kay snapped. "Go away."

But he was wrong. A shard of ice had pierced his eye, and another had lodged in his heart.

From then on, Kay changed. He ignored Gerda
and snarled at everything and everyone. He never
even smiled – until the day he saw a sleigh in the
street, driven by a beautiful lady. She invited Kay
to climb in with her. As they flew away, she gave
him an ice cold kiss.

After that kiss, Kay forgot all about his old life. But Gerda couldn't forget Kay. She missed her best friend terribly, so she decided to hunt him down – wherever he was.

With nothing to guide her, Gerda trusted to luck. She took a boat and floated down the river. The boat stopped by an old lady's cottage.

She told the old lady her story, but the old lady
was a witch! She was also lonely, so she tried to
trap Gerda in her house. She cast a spell and Gerda
forgot everything. For three months, Gerda lived
with the witch, quite happily, as if she'd always
lived there...

...but the witch couldn't
make the spell last.

Kay!

One day, it ended and
Gerda ran away.

By now, summer was over. Gerda walked a long way, until she had to rest, utterly exhausted.

"You look hungry and cold," croaked a raven.

"I can't stop." Gerda told the bird about her quest. "I miss Kay so very much."

The raven cocked its head to the side. "I've seen a boy who looks like that. He lives with the princess. They are married."

"Married!" said Gerda. "But Kay's too young."

"Our princess was looking for a husband," said the raven. "She met many fine kings and princes, but she didn't like anyone till a pretty boy showed up at the palace. It was a grand wedding..."

"I have to see him," said Gerda.

"That isn't so easy," cawed the raven. "The castle has high walls and burly guards...but I know a secret way in. Do you want me to show you?"

"Yes," said Gerda. "I wonder if he's happy?" Could it be Kay? She couldn't imagine her Kay married to anyone.

With the raven's help, Gerda found her way to the princess's bedchamber. She peered closely at the boy in bed. It wasn't Kay!

She burst into tears of relief. Her sobs woke up first the boy, then the princess. They both spoke at once. "Who are you? What are you doing here?"

Gerda explained her quest to find her friend. After hearing her sad story, the princess was greatly moved and wanted to help.

"Here's money, and warm clothes, and a golden carriage to help you on your way!" she said.

Unfortunately, the golden carriage carried Gerda into terrible danger. She was ambushed by a band of robbers, who jumped from the trees, howling.

"I'll have this little girl for my servant," cackled a smelly old lady, who dragged Gerda out.

"Hands off! She's mine," snarled a wild girl. The smelly woman was clearly scared of the girl and backed away, releasing Gerda.

"I'll ride with her back to our castle," said the robber girl. "She can be my new friend."

"What were you thinking?" the robber girl asked Gerda. "A golden carriage without any guards?"

They drove to the robbers' castle. It was huge and gloomy. The girl had a whole crumbling tower to herself, packed full of animals. Gerda looked around nervously, trying to see a way out.

"Do you like my birds?" said the robber girl, pointing to the cages that hung from the roof. "And this is my reindeer. His name is Ba. He wants to leave, but I love him too much to let him go."

As they went to sleep, the birds
began to sing sweet songs.

"Kay, Kay is far away!"
they trilled. "He went
away, in the Snow
Queen's sleigh."

Gerda listened,
with her heart
pounding.

"The Snow Queen lives in her palace in the Far North," said Ba, the reindeer. "That is my country."

"Can you take me there?" whispered Gerda.

"If I ever leave," answered Ba, a little sadly.

The robber girl overheard them talking and her heart melted with pity. Gerda deserved a chance.

"Dear Ba, you must carry Gerda away, to find her friend. I'll find you some food for the journey."

Gerda and brave Ba set off for the North.

Ba carried Gerda across mountains and cold rivers and through deep, dark woods. The days grew shorter and shorter until one morning the sun never rose at all.

"We have arrived in the Far North," said Ba.

"Look! There's a little house," said Gerda. "Somewhere warm to spend the night!"

An old lady lived in the house. She gladly shared her home with the weary visitors. As she fried up crispy ice-trout, she listened to Gerda's story.

"You are very strong," she said. "So strong and so very young!"

"I have good news for you...or maybe bad.
The North Winds sing of your friend. He lives in
the Snow Queen's palace now. Be wary! There are
shards of ice in his heart and his eye. So long as
they remain, he can never escape."

The next day, Ba carried Gerda towards the top
of the world, until he could walk no further.
A terrible snow storm raged about them.

Gerda battled through the snow. Icy beasts – the
Snow Queen's guards – swirled out of the storm
and attacked her with shivering fury.

"Leave me alone!" shouted Gerda. To her
astonishment, her frosty breath turned into angels,
who fought off the beasts and warmed her up.

Gerda crept into the palace. Pillars
of glittering crystal lined the way
into a shimmering chamber.
It was beautiful and terrifying
and very, very cold.

Gerda found Kay slumped
asleep beside the throne.
Weeping tears of joy,
she ran over and
hugged him tight.

Her hot tears melted the shards of ice in his
heart and eye. Kay blinked and smiled.

"Gerda, is that really you?" he said.

"Let's go home," said Gerda, utterly delighted.
She had her best friend back at last. They fled the
palace, and Ba, the brave reindeer, carried them
quickly south, away from the lands of winter.

"Where have you been?" said her grandma when they arrived home. "I'm so glad you are back!"

Outside the window, roses bloomed. Their sweet scent, carried on the warm summer breeze, whispered a promise of happy days to come.

THE MAGIC PEAR TREE

Long ago in China, there was a selfish and greedy man named Shen. Shen lived in a little house with a lush garden surrounded by stone walls. He built the walls himself, because he didn't want to share his garden with anyone.

Shoo!

Most of all, Shen didn't want anyone else touching his pear tree. It was just one tree, but it grew dozens of pears, which were sweet and juicy and as golden as an emperor's crown. Shen was convinced he could sell them for a fortune.

One bright day, Shen filled a wooden box with his pears and took it to sell in the town market. He smiled smugly when he saw the other stalls – none of their fruit or vegetables looked nearly as delicious as his prized pears. He was certain that his pears would sell in seconds.

Pears for sale!

The first customer who came to look was a disappointment – a beggar, with no money at all. The man looked hungry and had spied the ravishing pears. He reached for one, but Shen snatched it away.

"Can you pay for this?" Shen demanded.

"I don't have any money," the beggar replied. "But I'm very hungry, and would love a pear."

Shen snorted. He wasn't going to make his fortune by giving his pears away for free.

"One of these other stalls might give you their fruit," he snapped at the beggar. "But these are the sweetest pears in China. Come back when you have some money, or never come back at all."

A kind woman, who had been shopping close by, overheard Shen's rude words to the poor beggar.

"Can't you give that man one pear?" she asked.

"You have so many," she added, "and he has nothing."

"No!" spat Shen. "You can go away too. Unless, that is, you want to buy a delicious fresh pear?"

The woman surprised
Shen by bringing out
a purse full of coins.
"Actually, I will buy
a pear," she said.

She handed Shen
a coin and he gave
her the pear.

Instead of eating
it, she gave it to the
beggar. "I'm sorry
that man was so
rude," she said.

"You are kind,"
replied the beggar.
"Thank you."

The beggar was
so hungry that
he munched the
whole pear in five
quick bites.

"Yummy," he
spluttered. "This
truly is a tasty pear."

Once he had
finished, the beggar
spat out the pear's
black seeds into his
open hand.

"Ptoof!"

141

Clutching the seeds, the beggar turned and
bowed slightly to Shen and the kind woman.
The smile on his face suggested that he had just
come up with a clever idea.

"Now it is my turn to give you a pear,"
he announced, as his grin grew even wider.

Shen's face flushed as red as the apples on the stalls, and he jabbed the beggar with his finger.

"So you do have money after all," he seethed. "You could have bought a pear. You just wanted to get one for free."

"No," the beggar insisted. "You don't understand..."

"I do understand," Shen muttered, as he gathered with the other shoppers to watch the beggar. "I understand that this beggar is a no good cheat," he added with a sniff.

Curious shoppers edged closer to Shen and the woman, mumbling to one another. "What is the beggar up to?" one of them asked.

They watched as the beggar knelt down
and dug a small hole in the ground. Then he
dropped the pear seeds into the hole.

A moment later, a strange sort of magic
began to happen...

Dazzling red and yellow sparks crackled from
the hole in the ground, along with curls of pink
and blue smoke.

"May I have some hot water?" the beggar asked.
A tea-seller scuttled over warily. "I have hot tea,"
he said, handing the beggar a teapot.

Carefully, the beggar poured the hot tea into the hole with the seeds and the sparks and the smoke. And then...

"Look!" someone breathed.

The crowd gasped as a brown shoot rose from the hole. Tiny leaves sprouted from its top, as the shoot grew taller and taller...

...and taller and taller!

"It's a pear tree!" Shen blurted.

"It's magic," the woman sighed.

"And just look at those pears," Shen groaned. "They...they look even more delicious than mine."

The tree grew to its full height in just a few
seconds, and the beggar picked one of its gleaming
golden pears. He gave it to the kind woman.

"Because you were so nice to me," he said,
"I want you to have the first one."

The woman ate the pear. Its juice dribbled
down her chin. "It's the sweetest fruit I have ever
tasted," she declared happily.

After that the beggar gave a pear to everyone at the market, and they all agreed with the kind woman: these were the finest pears in all of China.

Even Shen got a pear for free. "It's horrible," he scoffed. "It's a terrible pear!"

But, secretly, he thought it was the best pear he had ever tasted, too.

While everyone was chomping into their pears, no one saw the beggar begin to hack down the magical pear tree.

Once the tree was chopped down, the beggar simply strolled away. No one saw him again.

Shen was the first to turn around. When he did, he gave a curious high-pitched squeak, like a furious mouse.

All of Shen's pears were gone, and their wooden box was chopped to pieces. For a moment, Shen just stared, his mouth hanging open and a baffled look on his face...

Then his cheeks turned bright red again, as he realized that he had been tricked.

"That crafty beggar!" Shen fumed.

"He turned my box into a tree by magic. All of those pears he picked were mine! No wonder they were so delicious." He glared at the crowd of shoppers and stall holders. "I want them all back, every single one of them!"

But the crowd just laughed. They were all pleased to see that Shen had been tricked.

"There are no pears left," the kind woman said. "And they were just as tasty as you said."

"Next time, perhaps you will be less selfish."

SLEEPING BEAUTY

There was once a king and queen who lived in a magnificent palace. They hosted feasts every week and were loved by everyone in the kingdom. Despite this, they were deeply unhappy.

All they had ever wanted was a child.

"Try not to lose hope," the king comforted his wife. "I'm sure we will have a child one day."

Together, they visited the wisest advisors in the land, but no one could help. The cradle in the nursery just sat there, cold, untouched and empty.

That is, until one
joyful day when a
rosy-cheeked girl was
born. The king and
queen were delighted.

They immediately sent out
invitations to the christening.
All the lords, ladies, dukes and
duchesses were invited.

So too were the seven
fairies of the kingdom.
"Dearest fairies," their
invitation read, "Will you
be the godmothers to our
beautiful daughter?"

At the christening, the queen cleared her throat to make an announcement. "My friends," she began, "thank you all for coming. It is with great joy that I name our wonderful child, Rosalind!"

The guests cheered, then headed to the Great Hall for a feast. Each fairy was given a golden plate and goblet, studded with sparkling diamonds and glowing rubies.

"WAIT!" screeched a voice. A fuming fairy rose from a billow of smoke. "Did you forget there are EIGHT fairies in your kingdom?" she snarled.

Terrified, the queen ordered a servant to bring in a golden plate and goblet, but there were only plain silver ones left. The fairy was furious. Everyone fell silent.

"Um, time for Rosalind's presents?" the king said, nervously.

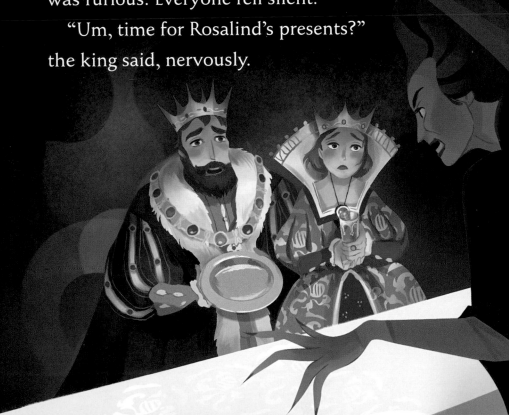

Six of the fairies flew over to the cradle to give Rosalind her gifts.

You will be kind...

clever...

graceful...

artistic...

musical...

a dancer...

Suddenly, WHAM! The beastly fairy
slammed down her hands
on the table and glared
at the princess.

"Baby Rosalind," she sneered, "you may be
clever, kind and talented, but you won't be for
long. At sixteen, you will prick your finger on
a spinning wheel and DIE!"

"Please, no!" the queen gasped, clutching the
cradle and bursting into tears.

The youngest fairy stood up. "Your majesty, please don't cry," she said. "I haven't given my gift yet. I cannot undo this wicked curse, but I can keep your child alive."

She pointed one finger to cast her spell. "Princess Rosalind, you won't die. You will sleep. After one hundred years, a prince will wake you."

On the king's orders, every spinning
wheel in the land was burned to ash...
except for one, which had been hidden.

Princess Rosalind
grew up just as the
fairies had wished.

She was clever
and artistic...

...graceful and kind.

One summer's day, just after
her sixteenth birthday, the king
and queen were away, and
Rosalind had nothing to do.

"I know," she thought,
"I'll explore the palace."

There were hundreds of tucked-away corners where nobody had been for years. Rosalind was climbing a dusty, winding staircase, when she came across a door to a room that she never knew existed.

Peeking inside, she saw an old woman, spinning wool.

"Hello, dear child, would you like a try?" the woman asked, and beckoned Rosalind over with one long, crooked finger.

Rosalind nodded. She'd never even seen a spinning wheel before.

Curious, she reached out to touch it...

But as Rosalind bent over, she pricked her finger on the needle and dropped to the floor.

"Ha ha!" crowed the old woman. "Let's see if the king and queen remember me now!" Cackling, she vanished in a thick puff of smoke.

Her piercing laugh echoed through the palace.
Servants heard and dashed towards the noise.
Eventually they found Rosalind asleep on the floor.
Alarmed, they shook her, but she didn't wake up.

"The fairy's curse!" one servant cried, after ten minutes of trying to rouse Rosalind. "It's come true."

Four footmen covered the princess in a soft, silk blanket and carried her to her bedroom.

The king and queen rushed home when they heard the awful news. "This can't be real," wailed the queen – shocked, forlorn and angry all at once.

The youngest fairy flew to the palace as soon as she could. She realized that, after a sleep of one hundred years, Rosalind would be lonely and confused when she woke up...

...so she sprinkled the whole palace with magic dust. The king, the queen, and all of their servants fell into a deep sleep on the spot.

Outside, trees and weeds entangled
the entire palace. A thick, icy fog
shrouded its walls. Only the tallest
turrets could be seen from afar.

The trees grew and grew into a thick,
dark forest, until there was no way through.

On a sunny day, one hundred years later,
a young prince was out riding his horse when
he spotted the palace in the distance. "Who
lives there?" he asked two passers-by.

"I heard it was a wicked troll!" said one.

"No, it's a sleeping princess!" said the other.

"Hmm…" the prince pondered, "I'm going to find out who's right." He sprang down from his horse and marched up to the misty, murky forest.

As he entered, the branches parted, creating a path. Lush leaves unfurled and pink roses burst into bloom. The prince strode on.

At the end of the path lay dozing dogs and slumbering spearmen. Anxious not to wake them, the prince tiptoed past.

He crept into the Great Hall, expecting to find
a fierce troll or an ogre. Instead, a king and queen
were fast asleep on their thrones.

"Could it really be true?" he wondered.
"Somewhere in this palace, could there really be
a sleeping princess?"

He explored further, until eventually he found...

...Rosalind, dreaming
peacefully in her bed.

"This can't be..." said the
prince in disbelief. He blushed
and took a deep breath, then
whispered, softly, "Princess,
can you hear me?"

Slowly, her eyes
fluttered open.

"Oh my..." she gasped, when she saw who was in front of her. "I've been dreaming of this moment for what feels like forever."

Rosalind smiled at the prince, who smiled back. "Princess," he began, "What happened here? Everyone is asleep!"

As he spoke, the rest of palace woke up.
At long last, the fairy's terrible curse had
been lifted.

Rosalind heard a murmur coming from the Great Hall. "My parents!" she cried, and ran downstairs with the prince to ask what had happened.

"The magic dust worked!" beamed the king, as they entered the hall. He told them the story from start to finish. The feast, the spinning wheel, the curse...everything. They were astonished.

The queen smiled at the prince. "Thank you for waking us. Stay in our palace whenever you wish."

He visited as often as he could. With every day that passed, he and Rosalind grew more in love.

One year later, they married and everyone was invited to their wedding – even the wicked fairy (just in case). But she was never seen again.

THE MAGIC PORRIDGE POT

Martha had no money and no one to look after her. She lived in a ramshackle old cottage, and her clothes were tatty and ragged. Much of the time, she went hungry. But when she did have some food, she was always ready to share it.

One day, she was
out for a walk when
she heard a buzzing.
"Bees," she thought.
"And bees mean...
HONEY!"

Carefully, so as not to upset the bees, she reached
into their hive and pulled out a piece of sweet,
sticky honeycomb, dripping with golden honey.

Then she heard
someone behind her.
It was an old woman
with a cooking pot.

"Hello," said Martha. She glanced at the pot.
There wasn't a trace of food inside it. "Perhaps
the woman is hungry too?" thought Martha.

"Would you like
some honey?" she
asked, breaking the
honeycomb in two.

"Oh yes," said the old
woman. "Thank you.
This will be delicious
with porridge."

"Let's try it!" the
woman went on.

"Um..." said Martha,
confused. "We don't
have any porridge."

"But we have my
pot," said the woman.

The old woman balanced the pot on a nearby stump. "This is no ordinary pot," she announced dramatically. "When I say the magic words, it will fill with porridge."

Martha looked at the
old woman. She looked
at the pot. She couldn't
see anything magical about it.

"She's crazy," thought Martha – but she was too
polite to say so. Instead, she said, "How clever!"

The old woman smiled. "Watch this," she said. "COOK POT, COOK!"

The pot shook ever so slightly and a tiny wisp of steam curled up from it. Martha's nose twitched. It smelled like...porridge!

The pot gave a shudder and then, to Martha's amazement, actual, hot porridge began to bubble up. In moments, the pot was full to the brim.

"I think that's enough," said the old woman. "Now listen, dear, this part is important... STOP POT, STOP!"

Immediately, the pot stopped.

Martha and the
woman sat down
to eat together.

The porridge was hot and sweet and delicious,
especially with the honey, and there was more
than enough for everyone. Martha thought she
had never felt so full and warm and contented.

"Well, time to go," said the old woman, getting
to her feet. "You can keep the pot. I think you
need it more than I do."

"Just remember the magic words," she called, as
she hobbled off, "and you'll never be hungry again!"

"I'll remember," said Martha. "Thank you!"

From that day on, Martha had plenty to eat. She had hot porridge for breakfast...

...fresh porridge, with porridge sauce, for lunch...

...and a large helping of porridge for dinner, with extra porridge for dessert.

One evening, a greedy boy was walking past
Martha's cottage when he smelled something hot
and sweet and delicious.

"Mmm," he thought,
sniffing the air. "Porridge!"

The boy followed the smell to the cottage.
Silently, he tiptoed up to the window and peeked
through. He watched Martha put the pot on the
table. He heard her say the magic words:

"COOK POT, COOK!"

He saw the pot shudder and start to fill with
fresh, steaming porridge, but...

...he didn't see it stop.

Martha drew the curtains and sat down to dinner, unaware of anything unusual.

"I WANT that pot!" thought the boy. He didn't care that it was Martha's. He watched until she went to bed.

Then he slipped inside her cottage, grabbed the pot and ran all the way back home, as fast as his legs would carry him.

He couldn't wait to try it out.
Eagerly, he said the magic words...

COOK POT, COOK!

The pot gave a shiver. It gave a
shudder. Hot porridge bubbled up
and a sweet smell filled the air.
The boy licked his lips greedily. At last, when
the pot was full to the brim, he said, "Stop."

But the pot didn't stop. Porridge dripped over the edge and fell in sticky great dollops on the table.

"Hey, I said STOP!" the boy cried, more loudly this time.

But the pot didn't stop. Now porridge was flowing thickly across the table and beginning to flood onto the floor. **Splurt! Splatter! Splat!**

"No-o-o," wailed the boy. "STOP – that's enough! No more!"

But the pot didn't stop. **Splurt! Splat! Splosh!** Before long, the floor had disappeared beneath a sticky sea of porridge.

HELP!

"STOP! STOP! STOP!" yelled the boy.
"Pleeease!"

But the pot didn't stop. **Splurt!**
Splash! Sploosh! Porridge began
to bubble out of the windows.

The boy waded out into the moonlit night.
A gloopy flood of porridge followed him
through the door and down the street.

And still the pot didn't stop. Slowly but surely, the porridge flood grew deeper and deeper and DEEPER.

"Help!" gasped the boy. "I'll drown in porridge!"

In her cottage,
Martha's nose twitched.
"That's funny," she
thought. "I can smell
porridge!" She glanced
out of the window –
and gasped.

There was a lake
of porridge around
the boy's house.
"It must be the
pot," she thought.
"I'd better do
something, fast!"
She raced
outside...

At the edge of the flood, she
stopped and raised her voice.
"STOP POT, STOP!"

And at last, the pot stopped.

The greedy boy was saved – but his house
was now surrounded by mounds of cold,
congealing porridge.

"How will I get home?" he wailed.

"I think you'll have to eat your way back,"
said Martha, trying not to laugh.

Urgh!

"Oh, and you had better
return my pot...when you
find it," she added.

It was too much porridge for the greedy boy.

"I'll never touch the stuff again," he told Martha the next day. "Here's your pot. Sorry for taking it."

Martha, on the other hand, never grew tired of her magical meals and lived happily ever after.

THE NUTCRACKER

It was Christmas Eve. Clara had never been
so excited. The night was filled with feathery
snow, and a special person had come to visit – her
godfather! Clara loved his visits; something magical
always seemed to happen when he was around.

"Merry Christmas Clara!" her godfather said, with a chuckle. He placed a package tied with a pretty bow under the tree. "I have a very special present for you this year."

That night, Clara was so full of Christmas joy that she couldn't sleep a wink.

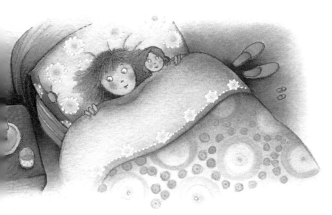

She was desperate to find out what was inside that package. She decided to sneak downstairs, and have a peek...

For Clara,
I hope this
protects
you...

Clara tiptoed down the stairs, being careful not to wake anyone in the house. Tingling with excitement, she crept to the tree and found her godfather's gift.

The message on its label was peculiar. "How could a present protect me?" Clara wondered.

Quietly, she peeled back the wrapping paper to reveal a wonderful wooden toy. It was a nutcracker doll, dressed in a soldier's tunic and a tall feathered hat.

The clock struck
midnight. As the chimes
echoed around the
house, Clara suddenly
felt tired. She found
a cushion, curled up
and fell fast asleep.

She woke with a curious
feeling... Something
unbelievable seemed to have
happened as she had slept.
Clara had shrunk!

It was incredible –
she was smaller than
the presents. Even
stranger, someone was
watching her from the
Christmas tree...

A tall figure stepped
from the branches.
It was her new toy –
come to life! "Don't
be afraid, Clara," the
toy said. "I am the
Nutcracker Prince."

The prince raised his sword, and more soldiers
marched from a toy box. "We're here to protect
you," he declared.

"Protect me?" asked Clara. "From what?"

Quick march!

"From *these* rascals!" the prince cried.

At that moment, several huge mice charged from the shadows, with wild eyes and razor sharp claws. Clara shrieked and hid behind the prince, as the soldiers fired lumps of cheese from a cannon, fighting off the attackers.

The danger wasn't over yet. Another mouse
burst from behind a present, waving a sword. The
creature wore a glittering crown and a sinister grin.

"It's the Mouse King," the prince breathed.

With a brave cry,
the prince leaped into
action. Their swords
clashed and clanged...

Just as the prince seemed to be driving the Mouse King away, he tripped on a lump of cheese, and tumbled back. The Mouse King seized his chance and pounced on the poor prince.

"Now I have you," he snarled, and his evil smile spread wider than ever.

Right at that moment, Clara struck too. She whipped off her shoe and hurled it as hard as she could at the Mouse King. It was a perfect shot, knocking the villain out cold.

Clara rushed to help the prince, whose face had flushed red with embarrassment. "In the end it was *you* who saved *me*," he gasped.

The prince whisked Clara to a golden sleigh waiting behind the Christmas tree, and they climbed on.

"Where are we going?" Clara asked.

"You'll see," replied the prince. He called to four reindeer to pull the sleigh. "Come on, boys!"

The reindeer galloped and galloped...and took off! They flew through a window, carrying Clara and the prince out into the frosty night.

They landed softly in a forest that glistened with fresh white snow. Clara knew immediately that it was a magical place.

"There is someone I would like you to meet," the prince explained, as he helped Clara down from the sleigh.

A lady swept from among the trees, dressed in a robe that was somehow brighter, whiter and more sparkling than the snow. Clara gasped. She was the most beautiful woman she had ever seen.

"This is my friend, the Ice Queen," announced the prince.

The Ice Queen led them to a palace carved
of ice so pure it looked like crystal. Its grand
doorway gleamed in the moonlight,
and its soaring towers reflected
the shivering stars.

Clara's eyes were wide with wonder as she followed the Ice Queen inside, where icicle chandeliers hung from arched ceilings.

"You arrived just in time," the Ice Queen said.

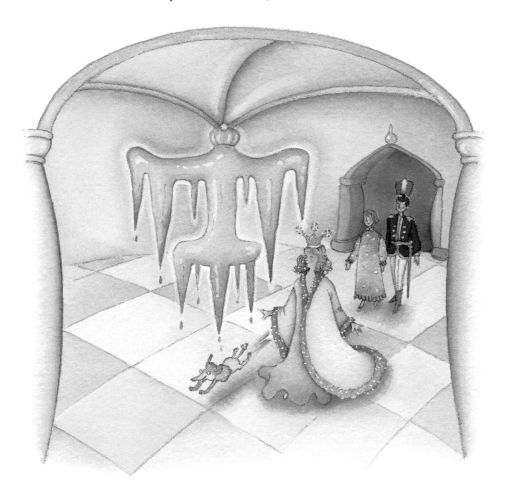

Eight ballerinas performed for Clara in the palace's grand ballroom. They seemed to float through the air like snowflakes.

After the dance, Clara played catch with the palace poodle. "I'll always remember this night," she told the happy little dog.

Clara didn't want to leave, but the prince
promised that their next stop would be even more
memorable. They flew away in their sleigh, waving
to the kind Ice Queen as they rose up into the
night and the snow.

Goodbye!

The prince was right – when they finally landed,
Clara could barely believe her eyes.

"Welcome to the Land of Sweets," said the prince.

Everywhere Clara looked she saw something
delicious. The trees were huge sticky
lollipops, and rivers of strawberry
milkshake cascaded down mountains
topped with melted chocolate.

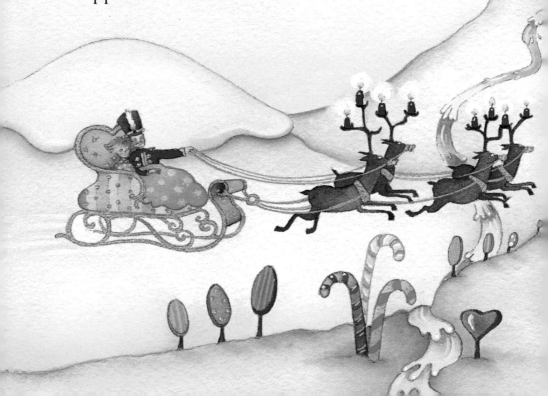

Most astonishing of all was a huge marzipan
castle covered with all kinds of
scrumptious treats.

As Clara and the
prince approached
the castle, a fairy
appeared, dressed
from head to toe
in pink. "I am the
Sugarplum Fairy,"
she cooed. "And
you are just in time
for our feast."

She led them to a
grand hall, where a long
table was crammed
with mouth-watering
delights – cakes, cookies
and candy swirls.

Clara and the prince sat on seats made of raspberry mousse, and they ate and ate and ate and ate.

After the feast, a band struck up at the side of the hall, and dancers from all over the world performed for Clara.

First came the dance of chocolate. Spanish dancers, in outfits studded with chocolate, spun around and snapped castanets.

Next, came the exotic dance of
coffee. Clara watched, mesmerized,
as an Arabian princess twirled
between cups of steaming coffee. The
music was slow and soothing, and the
dancer swirled like the steam.

The third group of dancers, from China, performed a lively tea dance. More and more dances followed, and Clara clapped and gasped at each.

In the final act, a group of ballerinas dressed as wild flowers danced a slow waltz for Clara. It was so beautiful that Clara thought she might cry.

At last, sadly, it was time to go home. With a happy sigh, Clara climbed back into the sleigh and waved farewell to the Sugarplum Fairy.

"It's been such a magical evening," she murmured to the Nutcracker Prince, before falling asleep on his shoulder.

When Clara woke, she was back under the Christmas tree, and the prince had gone. "Oh, it was all a dream," she realized, with a yawn.

But something made Clara wonder...
Had her godfather known that the
Nutcracker Prince would protect
her? Was that why he gave her
that wonderful present?
And why did her mouth
taste of...candy swirls?

"Maybe," Clara thought,
as music from the night
began to play again in her
head, "it wasn't just
a dream after all."

For Clara,
I hope this
protects
you...

ALICE'S ADVENTURES IN WONDERLAND

Alice was getting tired of sitting with her sister. She had tried reading her sister's book, but it didn't have any pictures. "And what is the use of a book without pictures?" thought Alice.

She was wondering whether to
make a daisy-chain when suddenly
a White Rabbit ran past.

Now, there is nothing remarkable
about that. Alice wasn't even surprised
when the Rabbit cried, "Oh dear! Oh
dear! I shall be late!"

But when the Rabbit took a watch out of its
pocket, Alice ran after it. For whoever saw a
rabbit with a pocket – or a watch? She was just
in time to see the Rabbit pop down a large hole.

In another moment, Alice followed, never once considering how she was to get out again. She found herself falling down a deep well, lined with shelves.

Down...down...down... Would the fall never end? Alice was daydreaming about her cat, Dinah, when *thump!* she landed on a heap of dry leaves.

Oh my ears and whiskers, it's late!

Not in the least hurt, Alice jumped up. Ahead, the White Rabbit was hurrying down a passageway. Alice was after him like the wind. Then he turned a corner and vanished.

Alice was left in a hall with doors on both sides. But every single door was locked. Just as she thought she was stuck there forever, she saw a glass table with a golden key on top.

The key opened a tiny door. Beyond it, was the loveliest garden Alice had ever seen, with bright flowers and cool, sparkling fountains.

Alice longed to go into the garden but she was far too big. "If only I could shrink," she thought.

Back at the glass table, Alice saw a bottle. She checked it carefully and, as it wasn't marked POISON, she took a sip. It tasted so delicious, she had very soon finished it.

"How curious," she said next. "I *am* shrinking!"

In an instant, she was small enough to fit through the tiny door – but she had left the key on the table out of reach. She was about to cry, when she noticed a cake.

"Curiouser and curiouser!" said
Alice, as she ate the cake and started
growing taller...and taller...
"Goodbye feet!" she called. "Ow!"
she added, as her head hit the ceiling.
Now she could easily reach the key, but
she was far too big to enter the garden.
Poor Alice. It was all too much and
this time she did cry. Huge, salty
tears splashed onto the floor
and formed a large pool.

She was standing in the
water when the White Rabbit
ran past, in such a hurry
that he dropped his fan.

Alice dried her eyes,
picked up the fan...
and found she was
shrinking again.

With a *splash!* she tumbled
into her salty pool of tears.

The pool was crowded with an assortment of birds and animals who had fallen in, too.

It was a very odd party that swam to shore, and all of them wet and uncomfortable.

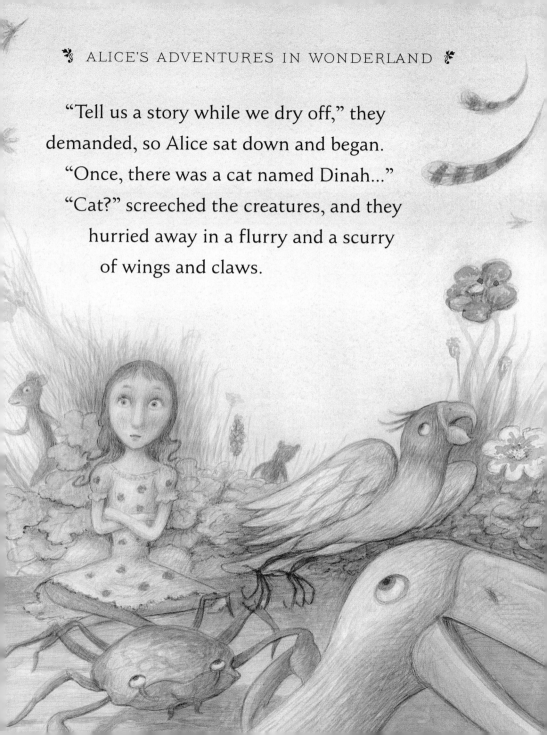

"Tell us a story while we dry off," they demanded, so Alice sat down and began.
"Once, there was a cat named Dinah…"
"Cat?" screeched the creatures, and they hurried away in a flurry and a scurry of wings and claws.

"Don't go!" called Alice, but she was left alone.
"Perhaps I'll look for that lovely garden," she
thought, and wandered along until she came to
a large mushroom. Sitting on top was a caterpillar,
quietly minding his own business.

The Caterpillar and Alice looked at each other.

"Who are YOU?" the Caterpillar
asked finally, in a sleepy voice.

"I hardly know," Alice replied. "I keep changing size and it's very confusing."

"What size do you want to be?" asked the Caterpillar.

"Larger than this," said Alice.

"Ah... Well, one side makes you taller, the other makes you shorter," the Caterpillar remarked.

"One side of what?" wondered Alice. "Oh, the mushroom!" She broke off a piece from each side and by nibbling first one and then the other, reached a size she liked.

Alice went on a little further. She was wondering where to go next, when a grinning Cheshire Cat appeared. "Please can you tell me–" she began.

"This way for the Hatter and that way for the March Hare," said the Cheshire Cat, pointing to two different paths. Alice was about to say more when he began to fade away.

"How odd!" she thought, picking a path at random.

A minute later, she came across *both* the March Hare and the Hatter, who were having tea together.

"Why is a raven like a writing desk?" the Hatter asked Alice.

"I don't know," she replied. "Why is a raven like a writing desk?"

The Hatter, who had paused to look at his watch, gave a shrug. "I've no idea," he said.

"Why are you wasting time asking riddles with no answer?" Alice wondered. "This is a ridiculous tea party!" she said to herself, and left.

"Well, I'll never go there again," said Alice, as she walked among some trees. To her surprise, she noticed one tree had a grand door in its trunk.

"That's very curious," she thought. "But everything is curious today. I think I'll go in."

She stepped through the door and came out...in the lovely garden at last – and face-to-face with the King and Queen of Hearts.

The Queen stared at Alice. "Off with her head!" she snapped.

"Nonsense!" Alice replied, in a firm voice.

The Queen was silent for a moment, before shouting, "Come and play a game with us, then."

Alice had never played such a strange game in all her life.

Everyone played at once, while the Queen stormed about, screaming, "Off with their heads!"

Alice was looking for a way to escape, when the Cheshire Cat appeared.

"Off with his head!" barked the Queen.

Instantly, the Cat's body vanished.

"Someone deal with this annoying cat," the Queen wailed.

The game carried on, with the Queen arguing with each player, until her guards had arrested nearly everyone.

"Time for the trial!" called a voice, suddenly.

Alice followed,
as everyone raced into
a crowded court room. She listened
closely as the crime was read out:
The Queen of Hearts, she made some tarts,
All on a summer day.
The Knave of Hearts, he stole those tarts
And took them quite away!

"Call the first witness!"
cried the White Rabbit.

It turned out to be the
Hatter, who walked in
still holding his tea cup,
and trembling so much
he couldn't speak.

As Alice watched, she
felt herself growing larger...

"He's useless!"
said the King. "Call
the next witness."

"Alice!" cried the
White Rabbit.

Alice stood up in
surprise and sent
the jury box flying.

"What do you know about all this?" asked the King of Hearts, his voice stern.

"Nothing," said Alice.

The Queen glared. "OFF WITH HER HEAD!"

"Nonsense!" Alice said, with a smile.

By now, Alice had grown to her full size. "You're nothing but a pack of cards!" she scoffed.

At this, the whole pack rose into the air and came flying down upon her.

Alice gasped...

...and woke to find her sister gently brushing a leaf from her face. "Oh, I've had such a strange and wonderful dream," said Alice, and she told her sister all about it, before running off for tea.

Designed by Laura Nelson Norris

Edited by Lesley Sims

Cover illustration: Lorena Alvarez

Digital imaging: Nick Wakeford

First published in 2018 by Usborne Publishing Ltd., 83-85 Saffron Hill, London EC1N 8RT, England. www.usborne.com. Copyright © 2018 Usborne Publishing Limited. The name Usborne and the devices ♀⊕ are Trade Marks of Usborne Publishing Ltd.